Africa meets India

By Anita Sax illustrated by Aija Jasuna

Publishers Cataloging-in-Publication Data

Sax, Anita.
    Africa meets india / by Anita Sax ; illustrated by Aija Jasuna.
        p. cm.
    Summary: An African elephant and an Indian elephant learn why there
is a difference in the size of their ears.
    ISBN-13: 978-1-60131-073-6
    [1. Elephants—Juvenile fiction. 2. Elephants—Africa. 3. Elephants—
India. 4. African elephant—Juvenile fiction. 5. Asiatic elephant.]
    I. Jasuna, Aija, ill. II. Title.

                                                    2010933059

115 Bluebill Drive
Savannah, GA 31419
    United States

Production Location: Guangzhou, China
Date of Production: November 2010
Cohort: Batch 1

This book was published with the assistance of the helpful folks at DragonPencil.com

In memory of my
loving mother

The summer morning sun twinkled blissfully through a canopy of massive trees in the jungle. Monkeys swung playfully from branch to branch as hungry giraffes munched on leafy greens.

Africa, the African elephant, arrived at the lake. She was eager to cool off from the heat. She put her life preserver and goggles on and sank her big feet into the water. As she dipped her long trunk and began bathing herself, she heard a voice behind her.

"Why are your ears so big?" the voice asked.

Africa stopped what she was doing. She wondered who on earth would ask such a thing. She turned around and was startled to find a smaller elephant standing right behind her. "Who are you?" asked Africa.

"I'm India," answered the other elephant proudly. "India, the Indian elephant!"

Africa took a good look at India and noticed that India's ears were much smaller than hers were.

"My ears are not too big," snapped Africa. "Your ears are too small!"

"That's not true!" cried India. "I'm five years old, and my ears are just right."

Africa couldn't believe India's response, for she was five years old too! This puzzled her. She couldn't understand why India's ears were smaller than hers. "But we are the same age," said Africa. "How come your ears are so small?"

"As I said before," replied India, who was now getting frustrated, "you are the one with gigantic ears!"

This annoyed Africa. She didn't like what India was saying. She filled her trunk with water and splashed India's face.

"What did you do that for?" cried India, shaking off the water.

"My ears are not too big," shouted Africa. "Your ears are way too small!"

A giraffe, who was chewing on
a branch nearby, heard the two
elephants arguing.

"Stop that!" he ordered.
"Both of you are wrong!"

Africa and India looked at each other in surprise and turned toward the giraffe.

"What do you mean?" asked India.

"It's simple," answered the giraffe, walking toward the elephants.

"We are both elephants and both the same age," cried Africa. "How come my ears are larger than India's?"

"Because," replied the giraffe, "you are an African elephant."

Africa looked confused. "What does that have to do with the size of our ears?" she asked.

"Well," explained the giraffe as he stretched his neck, "African elephants need larger ears, because Africa is a very large place filled with wide open plains. In Africa, the sun is very hot. There aren't many trees there to protect you from the heat. Therefore, you need larger ears to help you cool off."

Africa flapped her ears back and forth and giggled. "You mean like this?" she asked.

"That's right!" the giraffe chuckled.

"What about me?" asked India,
eager to know more.

The giraffe turned toward India. "Well," he said, "in India, where you come from, there are many forests filled with trees. The trees give you shade and protect you from the sun. Therefore, you don't need such big ears to cool off."

The two elephants stood side by side and compared each other's ears.

"He's right!" said Africa. "There aren't many trees where I come from."

"And where I come from, forests are filled with plenty!" said India.

"Don't forget," said the giraffe, "India is big, but Africa is bigger. Just like your ears, and that's easy to remember!"

The elephants waved their trunks good-bye as they watched the wise giraffe walk away.

They spent the rest of the day having fun playing together at the lake.